MEET
ABRAHAM LINCOLN

First paperback edition, 1989

Text copyright © 1965 by Random House, Inc. Illustrations copyright © 1989 by Stephen Marchesi. All rights reserved under International and Pan-American Copyright Conventions. Published in the United States by Random House, Inc., New York, and simultaneously in Canada by Random House of Canada Limited, Toronto.

Library of Congress Cataloging-in-Publication Data:
Cary, Barbara. Meet Abraham Lincoln / written by Barbara Cary ; illustrated by Stephen Marchesi.   p.   cm.—(Step-up biographies) SUMMARY: Highlights the life of the man who was president during the Civil War.
ISBN: 0-394-81966-7 (pbk.); 0-394-91966-1 (lib. bdg.)
1. Lincoln, Abraham, 1809–1865—Juvenile literature.   2. Presidents—United States—Biography—Juvenile literature. [1. Lincoln, Abraham, 1809–1865.   2. Presidents.]
I. Marchesi, Stephen, ill.   II. Title.   III. Series.   E457.905.C27   1989
973.7'092'4— dc19   [B]   [92]   88-19066

Manufactured in the United States of America   2 3 4 5 6 7 8 9 0

MEET
ABRAHAM LINCOLN

★ ★ ★ ★

By Barbara Cary
Illustrated by Stephen Marchesi

STEP-UP BOOKS

Random House · New York

1

Abraham Lincoln has been dead for more than 100 years. Yet each year, on February 12, Americans remember his birthday. He was one of the great presidents of the United States. Americans still remember what he said. They still read what he wrote. They remember the things he did as president. They say that, if he had not lived, the United States might be two countries today instead of one.

Abraham Lincoln was born in 1809. In 1809 the United States was still a young country. Its first president, George Washington, had been dead for only ten years. In 1809 there were only 17 states.

Eight of the states were in the southern part of the country. It was warm in the South. Cotton would grow there. Some farmers had big cotton fields.

They bought black men and women to work in their fields. They made the blacks their slaves. A slave had to do anything his owner told him to do.

Nine of the states were in the North. It was cold in the North. It was too cold to grow cotton. So people in the North did not own slaves. They did not need them. And they did not want them. They made laws against owning slaves.

In 1809 most of the land owned by the United States was still wild. But people were moving to this wild land. They were building new homes. And they were starting new states.

When Lincoln was elected president, there were 33 states. In 18 of them there were laws against slavery. In 15 states people could own slaves.

Abraham Lincoln was born in one of the slave states. It was the state of Kentucky.

The United States in 1860, when Lincoln was elected president.

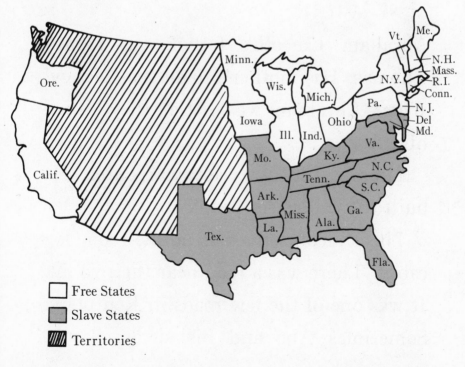

☐ Free States

■ Slave States

▨ Territories

2

Abraham Lincoln's father was named Thomas. His mother's name was Nancy. When Abraham was little, they called him Abe.

Thomas Lincoln was a carpenter. He built log cabins for people.

The Lincolns lived in a one-room log cabin. There was a road near their cabin. It was one of the few roads in Kentucky. Sometimes Abe and his sister, Sarah,

played by that road. Sometimes Abe just stood and watched people go by.

He saw families leaving Kentucky to start new states. He saw other families coming to live in Kentucky. Some of the white families had slaves with them. The families rode. The slaves walked.

Once Abe saw a soldier on the road. Abe had been fishing that day. He had caught a little fish. His mother had told him to be good to soldiers. He gave the soldier the fish.

Abe used the road to go to school. His school was in a log cabin. It was called a "blab" school because the children studied out loud. The noise they made sounded like "blab-blab-blab."

Abe could not go to school very often. But somehow he learned to read and write. His mother and father could not read and write. Not many country people could in those days.

Abe did not have paper to write on. He did not even have a pencil. He held a stick over a fire until the end was black. Then he wrote with it on a wooden board.

The only book he had was a Bible. Some of the words were hard. But he figured them out. He read the Bible over and over. Finally he knew most of the stories by heart.

3

When Abe was seven, the Lincolns left Kentucky. One reason they left was that another man said he owned their land. Thomas thought he owned the land. He had bought it. But the other man said he had bought it first.

Thomas did not have much money. He could not pay a lawyer to find out who was right.

Another reason the Lincolns moved was that Kentucky was a slave state. Thomas and Nancy did not like living in a state where people could own slaves.

Thomas went to another state, called

Indiana. In Indiana slavery was against the law. Indiana was a new state. Not many people lived there. In Indiana, Thomas could buy land from the government and be sure he owned it. And he did not have to pay for it all at once.

Thomas bought some land. It was at a place called Pigeon Creek. Then he went back to Kentucky to get his family.

It was winter when the Lincolns got to Pigeon Creek. While Thomas built a cabin, they lived in a shed made of branches. The shed was very small. And it was very cold. There was no room in it for a fire. Nancy and Sarah had to cook over an open fire outside.

Abe was a small boy. But he had to work like a man. He helped his father chop down trees to build their cabin. He helped him dig out tree stumps to clear a place to plant a garden in the spring. Abe once said that was the hardest winter he ever spent. "Those were pretty pinching times," he said.

4

After the first winter, things were better for the Lincolns. They had their cabin. Thomas and Abe had planted a garden. They bought some cows and pigs.

More people were moving to Pigeon Creek. An aunt and uncle of Nancy's came from Kentucky. They were Mr. and Mrs. Sparrow. The Lincolns were not as lonely as they had been.

At night the Sparrows often came to visit with the Lincolns. Abe loved to hear the grownups talk. When Abe could not understand their talk, he asked questions. His father said he asked too many questions. But Abe said he had to ask them. "There are so many things I want to know," he said.

Sometimes the grownups told stories. Thomas told stories about his childhood in Kentucky. When Thomas was a child, his father had been killed by Indians in Kentucky. This was a scary story. But Abe liked to hear about his grandfather and the Indians.

Sometimes Abe told stories too. They were funny ones that he made up. They made everyone laugh.

The Lincolns and the Sparrows had good times together. But the good times did not last. One fall a sickness came to Pigeon Creek. It was called "milk sickness." It came from drinking the milk of sick cows. Some of the Pigeon Creek people died from milk sickness. Mr. and Mrs. Sparrow died from it.

Then Abe's mother got the milk sickness. Thomas and Abe and Sarah took good care of her. They did all they could. But on a beautiful October morning, Nancy Lincoln died.

5

Abe and Sarah missed their mother badly. Thomas Lincoln missed her too. He hardly spoke. He never smiled. Sarah tried to cook and keep house. It was hard. She was only a little girl. Sometimes she sat by the cabin door and cried.

Abe hated to see Sarah cry. He tried to cheer her up. One day he brought her a baby raccoon to play with.

"He is nice," Sarah said. "But he is not the same as a mother."

Abe knew Sarah was right.

Nothing was the same without their mother.

For more than a year Thomas Lincoln and Abe and Sarah were sad and lonely. Then Thomas married again.

The new Mrs. Lincoln was a kind woman. She was a good wife to Thomas. She was a good mother to Abe and Sarah.

Abe loved his new mother. And she loved him. She said she could not have loved him more if he had been her own son.

A year after Thomas and Mrs. Lincoln were married, a school opened in Pigeon Creek. Mrs. Lincoln asked Thomas to send Abe to the school.

Abe was 11 years old. He was happy to go to school again. But he could not go as much as he wanted. He went for a few weeks. Then he stopped. Then he went for a few more weeks. Then he had to stop again. All the weeks added together came to less than a year. When he was grown up, Lincoln said, "I went to school by littles."

6

Sometimes Abe had to stop school to help his father on the farm. Sometimes he stopped because Thomas needed money. In those days any money a boy earned before he was 21 belonged to his father. Farmers paid Thomas 25 cents a day to have Abe work for them.

Abe worked hard. But he did not want to be a farmer. "My father taught me to farm," he once said. "But he never taught me to love it."

Abe did not like to farm. He liked to read. He began to borrow books. There were not many books in Pigeon Creek to borrow. But he borrowed all there were.

He read books at night by the light of the fire. One book he read was about George Washington. He read about how

Washington had helped the United States become a new country. Washington became a great hero to Abe.

Another book Abe read was a book of Indiana laws. It was not a very exciting book. But Abe liked it.

He learned that there were many laws. He wondered if a lawyer had to remember them all.

When Abe read, he seemed to be in another world. He did not even hear people speak to him. It made his father cross. Thomas did not understand why Abe wanted to read. Thomas said it was enough for a boy to work hard and be strong. He said Abe was wasting his time.

Mrs. Lincoln understood Abe better. She told Thomas to let him read. She said she thought Abe would be a great man someday.

"A great lazybones, if you ask me," Thomas said.

7

By the time Abe was 19, he was six feet four inches tall. He was the tallest boy in Pigeon Creek. He was the strongest boy too.

One day a farmer told Abe he had a job for a strong boy. His son, Allen, was taking some things to New Orleans to sell. He asked Abe to go along.

Abe was excited. New Orleans was in the state of Louisiana. It was a southern city. It was almost 1,000 miles from Pigeon Creek!

Abe said he would like to go to New Orleans. But he would have to ask his father.

The farmer said that he would pay Thomas eight dollars for each month Abe was away. That was more money than Abe had ever earned. Thomas said he could go.

Abe and Allen took the farmer's things to the Ohio River. They loaded the things onto a flatboat. Then they floated down the Ohio to the great Mississippi River.

New Orleans was at the very end of the Mississippi River. It took a long time to get there.

Abe had never been to a big city before. There were houses made of brick and stone. At first he thought New Orleans was a wonderful place. But then he saw a market where slaves were being sold. Abe did not like what he saw. And he was not unhappy when he and Allen had to start back to Pigeon Creek.

8

The year after Abe got back from New Orleans, Thomas Lincoln wanted to move again. He had heard the land was better in the state of Illinois. Abe helped his father move to Illinois. He helped him build a cabin to live in.

Then Abe said good-bye to his family. He was 21 now. And he could work for himself.

For a year he wandered about doing odd jobs. Then he went to live in a little town called New Salem.

New Salem was a pretty town. It was near a river. Abe lived there for six years. While he was there he had many jobs.

He worked in a store. The New Salem people said he was the most honest store-keeper they had ever had. But the store failed. There was a mill in New Salem. Abe worked at the mill. He ground corn into flour. He worked as a surveyor, making maps of people's land. For a while he was the New Salem mailman.

There was no post office in the town. When the mail came, Abe put the letters in his hat. Then he carried them to people.

When people in New Salem were asked where their post office was, they always said, "Our post office is in Abe's hat."

Abe made good friends in New Salem.

Everyone liked him. Ladies liked him because he was so kind and helpful. If a woman needed water from the river, Abe got it for her. If a woman needed wood for a fire, he chopped it. He even helped the mothers with their children.

He brought the children candy. He played with them. He rocked the babies to sleep. One mother said, "Abe Lincoln will do anything to help anyone."

9

The New Salem men liked Abe because he could tell funny stories. They liked him because he was good at sports and games. He could jump higher and run faster and throw a ball farther than any of them. They liked to talk to him too. They liked to talk to him about politics.

Once a week a newspaper came to New Salem. Abe learned about politics from the newspaper. He read what was being done in the Illinois state government. Then he told the New Salem men what he thought should be done. The men liked Abe's ideas. They said he should go into politics. Abe Lincoln liked the idea of going into politics.

In March of 1832 he said that he would like to be an Illinois state representative. As a representative he could help make the laws of the state. The people chose their representatives by voting. They voted for the men they liked best.

The next election would be in August. Abe knew that all of his friends in New Salem would vote for him. But he knew he needed more votes than that. He would have to talk to people in other towns. If they liked what he said, he would get the votes he needed.

But Abe did not have time to go to the other towns. A war started in Illinois. And Lincoln went to fight in it.

10

The war was against some Indians in the northern part of Illinois. The Indians were led by Chief Black Hawk. He said the Illinois people had taken some Indian land. Abe joined the Illinois army.

Some other young men from New Salem joined too. The New Salem men asked Abe to be their captain.

It was spring when Captain Abe and his men marched off to the war.

It rained every day. The men were wet and cold. The roads were muddy. The food for the army was in wagons. The wagons got stuck in the mud. The army had to leave the wagons behind.

Then the men had to hunt for their own food. Once Abe's men did not find any food for two days.

At last they caught an old hen. They cooked it over an open fire.

Abe said it tasted like a shoe. But he ate it. He was too hungry to care.

Abe and his men never fought the Indians. Black Hawk lost the war before they got to it.

When they came back to New Salem, some of the men told stories about how brave they had been. Abe just laughed. He said that he had been a great hero too. He said he had been wounded by thorns, and that he had killed lots of mosquitoes.

11

Abe now went back to politics. But there were only two weeks before the election. Abe could not get enough votes. There was not enough time. He lost the election.

But after two years there was another election. This time Abe had time to work for votes. He went to many other towns. He talked to many people.

He talked to them about roads. The roads in Illinois were very bad. Abe said that if he was elected representative he would vote for better roads. There were no public schools in Illinois. Abe said every child should have a chance to go to school. He said he would vote for public schools.

People liked what Abe said. In 1834 he was elected as one of the Illinois state representatives.

After Abe was elected, he was an important man. People began to call him Lincoln. Or Mr. Lincoln.

Mr. Lincoln had to go to the state capital to do his work as a representative. The capital of Illinois was a town called Vandalia.

Lincoln met representatives from all parts of the state in Vandalia. He found that many of them were lawyers. Lincoln had always wanted to be a lawyer. Now he had a chance. One of the representatives said he would help Lincoln become a lawyer. He gave him law books to read.

The representatives worked in Vandalia for a few weeks each year. Then they went home. Lincoln went home to New Salem. He took the law books with him. He studied very hard. He studied so hard that he taught himself to be a lawyer in a few months. He was a good lawyer. And people trusted him. They knew he would work hard to win a law case he thought was right. He would not take a law case he thought was wrong.

Once a man in the wrong asked Lincoln to take his case. Lincoln said no. He said, "All the time I was talking to the jury, I'd be thinking I was a liar. And I believe I'd forget myself and say it out loud."

Lincoln worked hard as a state representative, too. One thing he worked to do was change the capital of Illinois.

Vandalia was a small town. North of Vandalia there was a bigger town called Springfield. Lincoln felt that it would make a much better state capital.

Some of the representatives did not want the capital moved. The representatives voted. And Lincoln's side won! Springfield became the new capital. Now Lincoln left New Salem for good. He went to live in Springfield. There was more work for

a lawyer in the new capital. He opened a law office. It soon became a busy place.

One night Lincoln went to a party in Springfield. At the party he met a young lady named Mary Todd. He thought she was the prettiest young lady he had ever seen.

Abraham Lincoln asked Mary Todd to dance with him.

"Miss Todd," he said, "I want to dance with you in the worst way."

Mary Todd danced with Lincoln. Then she said, "Mr. Lincoln danced just the way he said he would. He danced in the worst way."

But Mary Todd did not really care how Lincoln danced. She liked him. When he asked her to marry him, she said yes.

12

Mr. and Mrs. Lincoln bought a nice house in Springfield. Sometimes Mrs. Lincoln scolded her husband about the way he behaved in the house. Mr. Lincoln liked to lie down on the floor when he read. He liked to take off his coat and tie at home. He also liked to walk around with his shoes off. He said this gave his feet a chance to breathe.

Mrs. Lincoln told Mr. Lincoln to sit up in a chair when he read. She told him to keep his coat and tie on. She said his feet did not need to breathe. They needed to have shoes on them.

She scolded him. But she loved him. "Mr. Lincoln's heart is as big as his arms are long," she said.

The Lincolns had four sons. One of them died when he was a baby. His name was Edward. The other sons were Robert and William and Thomas. Friends called them Bob and Willie and Tad. Mr. Lincoln called Thomas "Tad" because he moved as quickly as a tadpole.

Mr. Lincoln loved to play with his boys. When they were little, he carried them around on his shoulders. Sometimes he pretended to be a horse. He took them for rides in a little red wagon.

When they were older, Mr. Lincoln played ball and many other games with them. Sometimes they came to his office. While he worked, they climbed all over him. They played with his books. They used his pens for darts. They were often quite naughty. But Mr. Lincoln never thought so. He thought his boys were wonderful.

13

Abraham Lincoln was an Illinois state representative for eight years. But he wanted to do more in politics. In 1847 he got his wish. The people of his district elected him to represent them in the United States Congress.

Every district in every state sent a representative to Congress. These people met in Washington, D.C.

When Lincoln went to Washington, there were 29 states in the United States.

In 15 states it was against the law to own slaves. But in the 14 Southern states people could own slaves. And they did.

There was a slave market in Washington. Lincoln was against anyone's owning slaves anywhere. Congress could

not change state laws about slavery. But Washington, D.C., was not a state. It was the capital of the United States. Congress could make a law against having slavery in the capital. Lincoln thought it should. But he could not get Congress to do it.

While Lincoln was in Congress, America was at war with Mexico.

Lincoln thought the United States had started the war to get some land. And he said so. The people in Lincoln's district in Illinois did not like his saying this. They wanted the United States to have all the land it could get. They did not want Lincoln as their representative anymore.

Congressmen were elected for two years. At the end of two years Lincoln went back to Springfield. For the next five years he had no political job. He worked as a lawyer. But in 1854 something happened that brought Lincoln back into politics.

14

The United States owned some land called the Kansas-Nebraska Territory. In 1820 Congress had made a law saying no one could own slaves there. But in 1854 Congress made a new law. It said this territory could have slavery if the people there voted for it. The new law made Lincoln very angry.

Lincoln said it was wrong for Congress

to help slavery spread all over the United States. It was bad enough having it in the South. He began making speeches against the Kansas-Nebraska Act.

Another Illinois man began making speeches for the law. His name was Stephen Douglas.

Mr. Douglas was a senator. Lincoln had represented only one district in Congress. As a senator, Douglas represented everyone in the state.

In 1858 Lincoln ran for senator against Douglas. Before the election they had seven debates. First one man talked. Then the other. Thousands of people came to hear their speeches. They came in trains, in wagons, and on foot.

Douglas said he did not think slavery was wrong. He said he did not care if there was slavery in the Kansas-Nebraska Territory. "Let the people vote on it," Stephen Douglas said.

Lincoln said that people should not be allowed to vote on things that were wrong.

Lincoln said they did not vote on stealing. Or killing. Or other wrong things. "And slavery is wrong," he said.

Douglas was a small man. People called him the Little Giant. They called Lincoln the Big Giant. They said the debates were a battle of the giants. They called them the Great Debates.

15

Lincoln did not win the election for senator. Douglas did. But the Great Debates made Lincoln famous.

People all over the country talked about his speeches. Some people said Lincoln should run for president of the United States.

In 1860 there was an election for president. Lincoln and Douglas ran. So did two other men.

This time it was Abraham Lincoln who won on Election Day.

Lincoln's friends in Springfield were very happy. But Lincoln was serious, and a little sad.

Lincoln knew it would be hard to be president. The people of the North and South were angry at each other over slav-

ery. The people in the South were angry at him, too. They knew he was against slavery. Not one Southern state had voted for him for president.

Lincoln was elected president on November 6, 1860. But he would not become president until March 4, 1861.

Between November and March seven states in the South broke away from the United States. They did not want Lincoln as their president.

These seven states started their own country. They called it the Confederate States of America. They elected their own president. His name was Jefferson Davis.

They started a Confederate army.

The Confederate army began to take over the forts in the South. These forts belonged to the United States. But the Confederate States said the forts were on their land. And that they belonged to the Confederate States.

16

On the day Lincoln became president, he made a speech. He said both the country and the states would die without one another. He said the Confederate States were still part of the United States.

He said the South must give back the forts they had taken. But the Confederate States did not listen. They took still another fort. It was Fort Sumter in South Carolina.

Lincoln asked men to join the United States Army. This call for an army made four more Southern states angry. They broke away from the United States. There were now 11 states in the Confederacy. They were all slave states.

But four other slave states did not join the Confederacy. They believed, as Lincoln did, that the states should stay united.

The country was divided. Two great

armies marched against one another. And the war began.

One side was fighting to keep the states united. The other was fighting to have its own country.

The men who fought to keep the United States together called themselves Union men. They called the war a civil war. A civil war is fought between people of the same country.

The men of the South said they did not

belong to the United States. They had their own country now. They said it was not a civil war. It was a war between the states.

It did not matter what it was called. Thousands and thousands of people were killed. During the war Lincoln was always sad. Once, he said, "I do not think I will ever be glad again."

17

Soon the Union army was bigger than the Confederate army. And it had more guns. The people of the Union states were sure they would win the war in no time.

Their large army marched into the South. But the Confederacy had great generals. And in the first big battle of the war the Confederate army won a great victory. It was a terrible day for the Union.

Some Northern men wanted to give up the war. Now they saw that it could be a long war. No one hated the war more than Lincoln. He hated to have soldiers die. But Lincoln said the Union army must go on fighting. It must fight until the "United States" were once again united.

Lincoln saved all the soldiers' lives he could. Sometimes soldiers were shot for breaking army rules. Lincoln saved hundreds of these men from being shot.

"I always sleep better when I know I have saved some poor soldier's life," he said.

The soldiers loved Lincoln. They called him Father Abraham. And he loved them. When he met a soldier on the street, he took off his hat and bowed. He went to see soldiers who were in hospitals. He stopped by every bed. He talked to every soldier. He sent letters to the families of

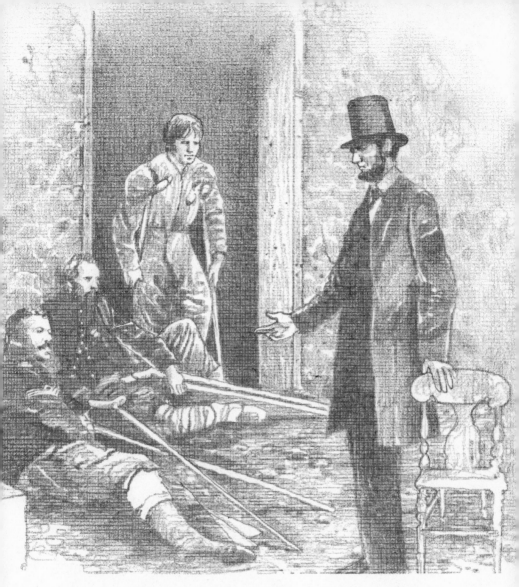

soldiers who had died. He told them how
sorry he was.

Mr. Lincoln knew how the families
felt. While he was president, his own son
Willie died.

18

As president, Lincoln had many problems. The Union generals were losing
battle after battle. He had to find better
generals. Another of his problems was
what to do about slavery. Many men in
the North were saying Lincoln should free
the slaves. Lincoln wanted to.

But the Union army needed all the help
it could get. Four slave states had stayed
in the Union. If the slaves were freed,

these states might join the Confederacy.

But something had to be done. Slavery had caused the war. Lincoln knew there could never be peace if the country was half slave and half free. He wrote a paper called the Emancipation Proclamation. This paper said that all the slaves in the Confederacy were free.

The Emancipation Proclamation did not put an end to slavery. The Confederacy went on fighting to keep its slaves. The slaves in the Union were still not free. But it gave a new meaning to the war. Now people felt that the war was not only to keep the states united. It was also a war for freedom.

In November of 1863 Lincoln gave a speech. In this speech he put both of these meanings together.

Lincoln gave the speech at Gettysburg, Pennsylvania. There had been a great battle at Gettysburg. The soldiers who had

died in the battle were buried there.

Lincoln spoke for less than three minutes. He said that the United States was a country of liberty. In it all men were created equal. And he said that the soldiers had died so that the United States might live.

It is one of the most beautiful speeches ever made. We call it the Gettysburg Address.

19

The Civil War lasted for four years. For two years the Union lost most of the battles. But at last Lincoln found generals who could win battles. One of the generals was Ulysses S. Grant. Lincoln made him the head of the army. Grant did not look much like a general.

He wore old clothes. He smoked big black cigars. But he knew how to fight.

Under General Grant the Union men

began to win battles. Now Lincoln knew he could do something more about freeing the slaves.

If the Union won the war, the Emancipation Proclamation would free the slaves in the Confederate states. But Lincoln wanted to free all the slaves. And he wanted to keep the people of the United States from ever owning slaves again. He wanted this to be a law for the whole country.

To make it a law in every state, Congress would have to vote for it first. Then the states would have to vote for it too.

In January of 1865 Congress voted for this law. Then the states began to vote. Lincoln hoped they would vote for the law he wanted.

In April, General Grant's army captured the city of Richmond. Richmond was the capital of the Confederacy. The next day Lincoln walked around the city. He saw the people who had been fighting him for so long. They watched him walk by. No one made a sound.

The Confederate army was small now. The men were hungry. They did not have enough clothes. They did not have enough guns. The Confederates knew they had lost. On April 9 General Robert E. Lee, the head of the Confederate army, surrendered to General Grant. The Civil War was over.

20

The month of April 1865 was a beautiful month in Washington. There were flowers in the gardens. There were new leaves on the trees. At last President Lincoln could be happy again. The long, hard war was over. One by one the states were voting to free the slaves. There would soon be no more slavery in the United States. And all the states would soon be united again.

On the morning of April 14 General Grant came to call at the White House. He said how well the President looked.

In the afternoon Mr. Lincoln played with his little son Tad. And he talked to his son Bob. Bob was just home from the army. Mr. Lincoln was glad to see his soldier son.

Then the President went for a ride with Mrs. Lincoln. She said he was happy that afternoon.

That night they went to a theater to see a play. It was a funny play. Mr. Lincoln laughed a lot. He was having a good time.

Suddenly there was a shot. At first the people in the theater thought it was part of the play.

But it was not. President Lincoln had been shot by a man who loved the Confederacy. Early the next morning President Lincoln died.

A train carried Mr. Lincoln back to Springfield. In town after town people stood to watch it go by. They could not believe their good and kind president was dead.

They knew he had loved them. And that he had loved his country, too. To keep his country united, he had taken it through a long and horrible war. And because of that war it had become a country where all people were free.

Today Americans still honor and love Abraham Lincoln for what he did more than 100 years ago.

THE
ENORMOUS
CROCODILE

ROALD DAHL

Pictures by Quentin Blake

SCHOLASTIC INC.

New York Toronto London Auckland Sydney
Mexico City New Delhi Hong Kong

To Sophie

ISBN 0-590-01869-8

27 26 25 24 23 22 21   4 5 6 7/0

Printed in the U.S.A.   08

First Scholastic printing, January 1998

In the biggest brownest muddiest river in Africa, two crocodiles lay with their heads just above the water. One of the crocodiles was enormous. The other was not so big.

"Do you know what I would like for my lunch today?" the Enormous Crocodile asked.

"No," the Notsobig One said. "What?"

The Enormous Crocodile grinned, showing hundreds of sharp white teeth. "For my lunch today," he said, "I would like a nice juicy little child."

"I never eat children," the Notsobig One said. "Only fish."

"Ho, ho, ho!" cried the Enormous Crocodile. "I'll bet if you saw a fat juicy little child paddling in the water over there at this very moment, you'd gulp him up in one gollop!"

"No, I wouldn't," the Notsobig One said. "Children are too tough and chewy. They are tough and chewy and nasty and bitter."

"*Tough* and *chewy*!" cried the Enormous Crocodile. "*Nasty* and *bitter*! What awful tommy-rot you talk! They are juicy and yummy!"

"They taste so bitter," the Notsobig One said, "you have to cover them with sugar before you can eat them."

"Children are bigger than fish," said the Enormous Crocodile. "You get bigger helpings."

"You are greedy," the Notsobig One said. "You're the greediest croc in the whole river."

"I'm the bravest croc in the whole river," said the Enormous Crocodile. "I'm the only one who dares to leave the water and go through the jungle to the town to look for little children to eat."

"You've only done that once," snorted the Notsobig One. "And what happened then? They all saw you coming and ran away."

"Ah, but today when I go, they won't see me at all," said the Enormous Crocodile.

"Of course they'll see you," the Notsobig One said. "You're so enormous and ugly, they'll see you from miles away."

The Enormous Crocodile grinned again, and his terrible sharp teeth sparkled like knives in the sun. "Nobody will see me," he said, "because this time I've thought up secret plans and clever tricks."

"Clever tricks?" cried the Notsobig One. "You've never done anything clever in your life! You're the stupidest croc in the whole river!"

"I'm the cleverest croc in the whole river," the Enormous Crocodile answered. "For my lunch today I shall feast upon a fat juicy little child while you lie here in the river feeling hungry. Goodbye."

The Enormous Crocodile swam to the side of the river, and crawled out of the water.

A gigantic creature was standing in the slimy oozy mud on the riverbank. It was Humpy-Rumpy the Hippopotamus.

"Hello, hello," said Humpy-Rumpy. "Where on earth are you off to at this time of day?"

"I have secret plans and clever tricks," said the Crocodile.

"Oh dear," said Humpy-Rumpy. "I'll bet you're going to do something horrid."

The Enormous Crocodile grinned at Humpy-Rumpy and said:

> *"I'm going to fill my hungry empty tummy*
> *With something yummy yummy yummy*
> *yummy!"*

"What's so yummy?" asked Humpy-Rumpy.

"Try to guess," said the Crocodile. "It's something that walks on two legs."

"You don't mean . . ." said Humpy-Rumpy. "You don't *really* mean you're going to eat a little child?"

"Of course I am," said the Crocodile.

"Oh, you horrid greedy grumptious brute!" cried Humpy-Rumpy. "I hope you get caught and cooked and turned into crocodile soup!"

The Enormous Crocodile laughed out loud at Humpy-Rumpy. Then he waddled off into the jungle.

Inside the jungle, he met Trunky the Elephant. Trunky was nibbling leaves from the top of a tall tree, and he didn't notice the Crocodile at first. So the Crocodile bit him on the leg.

"Ow!" said Trunky in his big deep voice. "Who did that? Oh, it's you, is it, you beastly Crocodile. Why don't you go back to the big brown muddy river where you belong?"

"I have secret plans and clever tricks," said the Crocodile.

"You mean you've got *nasty* plans and *nasty* tricks," said Trunky. "You've never done a nice thing in your life."

The Enormous Crocodile grinned up at Trunky and said:

*"I'm off to find a yummy child for lunch.
Keep listening and you'll hear the bones go
crunch!"*

"Oh, you wicked beastly beast!" cried Trunky. "Oh, you foul and filthy fiend! I hope you get squashed and squished and squizzled and boiled up into crocodile stew!"

The Enormous Crocodile laughed out loud and disappeared into the thick thick jungle.

A bit farther on, he met Muggle-Wump the Monkey. Muggle-Wump was sitting in a tree, eating nuts.

"Hello, Crocky," said Muggle-Wump. "What are you up to now?"

"I have secret plans and clever tricks," said the Crocodile.

"Would you like some nuts?" asked Muggle-Wump.

"I have better things to eat than nuts," sniffed the Crocodile.

"I didn't think there *was* anything better than nuts," said Muggle-Wump.

"Ah-ha," said the Enormous Crocodile,

> *"The sort of things that I am going to eat*
> *Have fingers, toe-nails, arms and legs and*
> *feet!"*

Muggle-Wump went pale and began to shake all over. "You aren't really going to gobble up a little child, are you?" he said.

"Of course I am," said the Crocodile. "Clothes and all. They taste better with the clothes on."

"Oh, you horrid hoggish croc!" cried Muggle-Wump. "You slimy creepy creature! I hope the buttons and buckles all stick in your throat and choke you to death!"

The Crocodile grinned up at Muggle-Wump and said, "I eat monkeys, too." And quick as a flash, with one bite of his huge jaws, he bit through the tree that Muggle-Wump was sitting in, and down it came. But just in time, Muggle-Wump jumped into the next tree and swung away through the branches.

A bit farther on, the Enormous Crocodile met the Roly-Poly Bird. The Roly-Poly Bird was building a nest in an orange tree.

"Hello there, Enormous Crocodile!" sang the Roly-Poly Bird. "We don't often see you up here in the jungle."

"Ah," said the Crocodile. "I have secret plans and clever tricks."

"I hope it's not something nasty," sang the Roly-Poly Bird.

"Nasty!" cried the Crocodile. "Of course it's not nasty! It's delicious!

"It's luscious, it's super,
It's mushious, it's duper,
It's better than rotten old fish.
You mash it and munch it,
You chew it and crunch it!
It's lovely to hear it go squish!"

"It must be berries," sang the Roly-Poly Bird. "Berries are my favorite food in the world. Is it raspberries, perhaps? Or could it be strawberries?"

The Enormous Crocodile laughed so much his teeth rattled together like pennies in a piggy bank. "Crocodiles don't eat berries," he said. "We eat little boys and girls. And sometimes we eat Roly-Poly Birds, as well." Very quickly, the Crocodile reached up and snapped his jaws at the Roly-Poly Bird. He just missed the Bird, but he managed to catch hold of the long beautiful feathers in its tail. The Roly-Poly Bird gave a shriek of terror and shot straight up into the air, leaving its tail feathers behind in the Enormous Crocodile's mouth.

At last, the Enormous Crocodile came out of the other side of the jungle into the sunshine. He could see the town not far away.

"Ho-ho!" he said, talking aloud to himself. "Ha-ha! That walk through the jungle has made me hungrier than ever. One child isn't going to be nearly enough for me today. I won't be full up until I've eaten at least three juicy little children!"

He started to creep forward toward the town.

The Enormous Crocodile crept over to a place where there were a lot of coconut trees.

He knew that children from the town often came here looking for coconuts. The trees were too tall for them to climb, but there were always some coconuts on the ground that had fallen down.

The Enormous Crocodile quickly collected all the coconuts that were lying on the ground. He also gathered together several fallen branches.

"Now for Clever Trick Number One!" he whispered to himself. "It won't be long before I am eating the first part of my lunch!"

He took all the coconut branches and held them between his teeth.

He grasped the coconuts in his front paws. Then he stood straight up in the air, balancing himself on his tail.

He had arranged the branches and the coconuts so cleverly that he now looked exactly like a small coconut tree standing among all the big coconut trees.

Soon, two children came along. They were brother and sister. The boy was called Toto. His sister was called Mary. They walked around looking for fallen coconuts, but they couldn't find any because the Enormous Crocodile had gathered them all up.

"Oh look!" cried Toto. "That tree over there is much smaller than the others! And it's full of coconuts! I think I could climb that one quite easily if you help me up the first part."

Toto and Mary ran toward what they thought was the small coconut tree.

The Enormous Crocodile peered through the branches, watching them as they came closer and closer. He licked his lips. He began to dribble with excitement.

Suddenly there was a tremendous whooshing noise. It was Humpy-Rumpy the Hippopotamus. He came crashing and snorting out of the jungle. His head was down low and he was galloping at a terrific speed.

"Look out, Toto!" shouted Humpy-Rumpy. "Look out, Mary! That's not a coconut tree! It's the Enormous Crocodile and he wants to eat you up!"

Humpy-Rumpy charged straight at the Enormous Crocodile. He caught him with his giant head and sent him tumbling and skidding over the ground.

"Ow-eeee!" cried the Crocodile. "Help! Stop! Where am I?"

Toto and Mary ran back to the town as fast as they could.

But crocodiles are tough. It is difficult for even a hippopotamus to hurt them.

The Enormous Crocodile picked himself up and crept toward the place where the children's playground was.

"Now for Clever Trick Number Two!" he said to himself. "This one is certain to work!"

There were no children in the playground at that moment. They were all in school.

The Enormous Crocodile found a big log and placed it in the middle of the playground. Then he lay across the log and tucked in his feet so that he looked almost exactly like a seesaw.

When school was over, the children all came running into the playground.

"Oh look!" they cried. "We've got a new seesaw!"

They all crowded around, shouting with excitement.

"I'll go first!"

"I'll get on the other end!"

"I want to go first!"

"So do I! So do I!"

Then, a girl who was older than the others said, "It's rather a funny knobbly sort of a seesaw, isn't it? Do you think it'll be safe to sit on!"

"Of course it will!" the others said. "It looks strong as anything!"

The Enormous Crocodile opened one eye just a tiny bit and watched the children who were crowding around him. Soon, he thought, one of them is going to sit on my head, then I will give a jerk and a snap, and after that it will be *yum yum yum*.

At that moment, there was a flash of brown and something jumped into the playground and hopped up onto the top of the swings.

It was Muggle-Wump the Monkey.

"Run!" Muggle-Wump shouted to the children. "All of you run, run, run! That's not a seesaw! It's the Enormous Crocodile and he wants to eat you up!"

The children screamed and ran for their lives.
Muggle-Wump disappeared back into the jungle,
and the Enormous Crocodile was left all alone in the
playground.

He cursed the Monkey and waddled back into the bushes to hide.

"I am getting hungrier and hungrier!" he said. "I shall have to eat at least four children now before I am full up!"

The Enormous Crocodile crept around the edge of the town, taking great care not to be seen.

He came to a place where they were getting ready to have a fair. There were slides and swings and dodgem-cars and people selling popcorn and cotton candy. There was also a big merry-go-round.

The merry-go-round had marvelous wooden creatures for the children to ride on. There were white horses and lions and tigers and mermaids with fish tails and fearsome dragons with red tongues sticking out of their mouths.

"Now for Clever Trick Number Three," said the Enormous Crocodile, licking his lips.

When no one was looking, he crept up onto the merry-go-round and put himself between a wooden lion and a fearsome dragon. He sat up a bit on his back legs and he kept very still. He looked exactly like a wooden crocodile on the merry-go-round.

Soon all sorts of children came flocking into the fair. Several of them ran toward the merry-go-round. They were very excited.

"I'm going to ride on a dragon!" cried one.

"I'm going on a lovely white horse!" cried another.

"I'm going on a lion!" cried a third one.

And one little girl, whose name was Jill, said, *"I'm going to ride on that funny old wooden crocodile!"*

The Enormous Crocodile kept very still, but he could see the little girl coming toward him. "Yummy-yum-yum," he thought. "I'll gulp her up easily in one gollop."

Suddenly there was a *swish* and a *swoosh* and something came swishing and swooshing out of the sky.

It was the Roly-Poly Bird.

He flew round and round the merry-go-round, singing, "Look out, Jill! Look out! Look out! Don't ride on that crocodile!"

Jill stopped and looked up.

"That's not a wooden crocodile!" sang the Roly-Poly Bird. "It's a real one! It's the Enormous Crocodile from the river and he wants to eat you up!"

Jill turned and ran. So did all the other children. Even the man who was working the merry-go-round jumped off it and ran away as fast as he could.

The Enormous Crocodile cursed the Roly-Poly Bird and waddled back into the bushes to hide.

"I am so hungry now," he said to himself, "I could eat six children before I am full up!"

Just outside the town, there was a pretty little field with trees and bushes all around it. This was called The Picnic Place. There were several wooden tables and long benches, and people were allowed to go there and have a picnic at any time.

The Enormous Crocodile crept over to The Picnic Place. There was no one in sight.

"Now for Clever Trick Number Four!" he whispered to himself.

He picked a lovely bunch of flowers and arranged it on one of the tables.

From the same table, he took away one of the benches and hid it in the bushes.

Then he put himself in the place where the bench had been.

By tucking his head under his chest, and by twisting his tail out of sight, he made himself look very much like a long wooden bench with four legs.

Soon, two boys and two girls came along carrying baskets of food. They were all from one family, and their mother had said they could go out and have a picnic together.

"Which table shall we sit at?" said one.

"Let's take the table with the lovely flowers on it," said another.

The Enormous Crocodile kept as quiet as a mouse. "I shall eat them all," he said to himself. "They will come and sit on my back and I will swizzle my head around quickly, and after that it'll be *squish crunch gollop*."

Suddenly a big deep voice from the jungle shouted, "Stand back children! Stand back! Stand back!"

The children stopped and stared at the place where the voice was coming from.

Then, with a crashing of branches, Trunky the Elephant came rushing out of the jungle.

"That's not a bench you were going to sit on!" he bellowed. "It's the Enormous Crocodile, and he wants to eat you all up!"

Trunky trotted over to the spot where the Enormous Crocodile was standing, and quick as a flash he wrapped his trunk round the Crocodile's tail and hoisted him up into the air.

"Hey! Let me go!" yelled the Enormous Crocodile, who was now dangling upside down. "Let me go! Let me go!"

"No," Trunky said. "I will not let you go. We've all had quite enough of your clever tricks."

Trunky began to swing the Crocodile round and round in the air. At first he swung him slowly.
Then he swung him faster . . .

And *faster* . . .
And FASTER . . .

And FASTER STILL . . .
Soon the Enormous Crocodile was just a blurry circle going round and round Trunky's head.

Suddenly, Trunky let go of the Crocodile's tail, and the Crocodile went shooting high up into the sky like a huge green rocket.

Up and up he went . . .

Higher and higher . . .

Faster and faster . . .

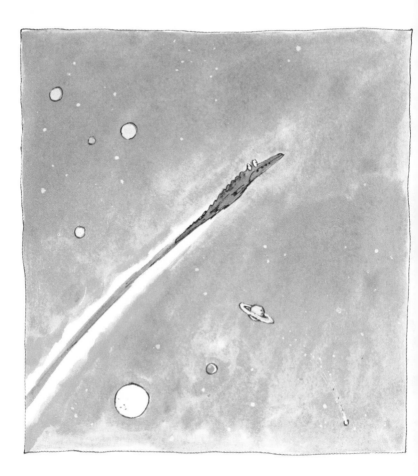

He was going so fast and so high that soon the earth was just a tiny dot miles below.

He whizzed on and on.

He whizzed far into space.

He whizzed past the moon.

He whizzed past stars and planets.

Until at last . . .

BANG

With the most tremendous
the Enormous Crocodile crashed headfirst into the
hot hot sun.
    And he was sizzled up like a sausage!